eLove
The Internet Dating Musical

Book, Music & Lyrics by
Wayland Pickard

Additional Lyrics by Sherry Netherland
and Deborah Johnson

A SAMUEL FRENCH ACTING EDITION

SAMUEL
FRENCH
FOUNDED 1830

NEW YORK HOLLYWOOD LONDON TORONTO
SAMUELFRENCH.COM

RENTAL MATERIALS

An orchestration consisting of a **Vocal Score** (Lead Sheets), a **rehearsal CD** and a **performance CD** will be loaned two months prior to the production ONLY on the receipt of the Licensing Fee quoted for all performances, the rental fee and a refundable deposit.

Please contact Samuel French for perusal of the music materials as well as a performance license application.

IMPORTANT BILLING AND CREDIT
REQUIREMENTS

All producers of *eLOVE* must give credit to the Author of the Play in all programs distributed in connection with performances of the Play, and in all instances in which the title of the Play appears for the purposes of advertising, publicizing or otherwise exploiting the Play and/or a production. The name of the Author *must* appear on a separate line on which no other name appears, immediately following the title and *must* appear in size of type not less than fifty percent of the size of the title type. However, "Additional Lyrics" name credits are to be fifty percent smaller than author credits.

In addition the following credit *must* be given in all programs and publicity information distributed in association with this piece:

eLove
The Internet Dating Musical
Book, Music & Lyrics by
Wayland Pickard

Additional Lyrics by
Sherry Netherland & Deborah Johnson

"eLove" The Internet Dating Musical, was first presented at the Lonny Chapman Group Repertory Theatre in North Hollywood, California on October 11, 2008. It was directed by Wayland Pickard. The choreography was by Stan Mazin, the sets were designed by Chris Winfield and technical direction was by Kate Shaw. The production consultant was Richard Alan Woody. Promotion and press was done by Laura Coker of Angry Amish Productions. A later production in 2009 was directed by Cate Caplin. Orchestrations, arrangements and recorded soundtracks were written and performed by Wayland Pickard. The cast was as follows:

CAROL . . . . Bobbi Stamm

FRANK. . . . . .Lloyd Pedersen

CHARACTERS

CAROL – Any age from 30-60+. Recently single and searching for true love on the internet, she is charming but lonely and works as a restaurant hostess. Returning from work, she is wearing casual attire.

FRANK – Can be of any *matching* age range from 30-60+. (*References to age can be altered in script according to cast.*) Frank is also recently single and searching for true love on the internet. He is witty but self-deprecating and works as a bookkeeper. Also returning from work, he is wearing a sports coat and tie.

SETTING

Two apartments

TIME

The present

ACT I
The time is the present in the two separate apartments of Carol and Frank. It is early evening on a Saturday night.

ACT II
Same apartments later that night and early Sunday morning.

MUSICAL NUMBERS

ACT I

"LOVE HAS A BRAND NEW DAY" .... (instrumental)

"I'M SINGLE"................................Carol & Frank

"PITY PARTY"................................Carol & Frank

"YOU'VE GOT MAIL" ....Carol & Frank

"WE'RE ALREADY THERE"....................Carol & Frank

"MY EX" ....Carol & Frank

ACT II

"IT'S ALL YOUR FAULT"......................Carol & Frank

"YOU NEVER LISTEN".............................. Carol

"IF WE HAD STAYED TOGETHER" ....Carol & Frank

"I WAS MEANT FOR YOU" ....Frank

"SO NEAR YET SO FAR AWAY"....................... .Carol

"LOVE HAS A BRAND NEW DAY" ....Frank & Carol

"I'M SINGLE"(REPRISE) ....Carol & Frank

"MY EX" (REPRISE) ....Carol & Frank

ACT I

(The time is the present. The place is two separate apartments that occupy either side of the stage separated by a short wall and a painted line along center stage. The décor suggests two apartments in different locations.)

(CAROL's tidy apartment is stage right and decorated in a modest but tasteful décor. Downstage, it has a framed movie poster of a Fred Astaire/Ginger Rogers movie classic. Stage left is FRANK's messy bachelor apartment. Piles of papers litter his bookshelves and desk. He has a framed Dixieland Jazz poster downstage left. Upstage left and right are front doors to each apartment. Further downstage left and right are exits to their unseen, offstage kitchens. On either side of center stage are computer desks with closed laptop computers. On CAROL's desk is a small fish bowl with one goldfish [a fake fish can be used]. On FRANK's computer desk is a turtle terrarium or bowl containing a large, very sedentary turtle [a painted prop or turtle shell can be used.] Both "pets" allow the actors to speak their thoughts out loud as a sounding board. Both desks have computer chairs with wheels that can be easily rolled around the stage. Casual work wardrobe suggests they have just returned home from their jobs. FRANK is a bookkeeper and CAROL is a hostess/assistant manager at a restaurant. They get into comfy robes as the story unfolds.)

(FRANK and CAROL are two lonely singles, both having recently experienced a bitter end to a

disastrous previous relationship. Disillusioned and cynical about love, they are living out their romantic dreams vicariously in cyberspace, desperately searching for true love and their perfect match using the internet dating scene. They're roaming for romance on a dating website after recently ending previous relationships. The two characters speak to each other over the internet, reading aloud their email messages at their computer desks, occasionally moving their wireless laptops off the desks to easy chairs downstage right and left. They only encounter each other in person during three brief flashback scenes in downstage center specials in front of the set. They both also leave their computer desks to go into offstage kitchen areas or to wander around their apartments speaking their private thoughts aloud.)

*(**Author's note:** This musical can also be presented as a continuous one-act without intermission. Cast members sing along to pre-recorded CD music tracks throughout.)*

(Overture music segues into the first scene and continues vamping as the stage lights up. **FRANK** *and* **CAROL** *enter their respective apartments through their upstage front doors on opposite sides of the stage.)*

*(**"PRE-SHOW MUSIC" – TRACK #1 (4:09)** HOUSE LIGHTS OUT.* ***CUE TRACK #2 OVERTURE/INTRO TO "I'M SINGLE"*** *STAGE LIGHTS UP.)*

*(**CAROL** enters her apartment upstage right and slams the door shut. She puts mail and groceries down and takes cellphone out of purse. She looks tired.)*

CAROL. *(speaking to her fish)* Whew! What a day at work. Another day of pointless futility…and no one to share all that misery with!

(**FRANK** *enters his apartment upstage left with briefcase, a bag of groceries and folded overcoat. He slams the door shut.*)

FRANK. *(speaking to his pet turtle)* Sometimes I just hate my job!...Can't wait to relax, all *alone* in my...

(looks pitifully around at the lonely solitude)

...over-priced singles apartment.

(**FRANK** *begins to unload groceries and briefcase.*)

CAROL. Now that I'm single again, it's the end of another long day...and the beginning of another lonely night.

(**CAROL** *and* **FRANK** *sing.*)

"I'M SINGLE"
(A SINGLE SONG)

CAROL.

I'M SINGLE...OH, GAWD, I'M SINGLE.
FORMERLY SOCIALITE,
ALONE ON A SATURDAY NIGHT.

FRANK.

I'M SINGLE...I NEED TO MINGLE.
SHARING EMO-T'NAL SCARS,
KISSING GOODNIGHT IN PARKED CARS.

CAROL.

MY LIFE IS NOW MY OWN
I FEEL EACH MINUTE IS SACRED.

FRANK.

EATING TAKE-OUT, RENTING MOVIES
DANCE AROUND NAKED.

CAROL.

TV OF MY CHOOSING,
NO MORE MONDAY NIGHT FOOTBALL.

FRANK.

MUSIC THAT FEEDS MY SOUL.

CAROL.

GOT THE REMOTE CONTROL!

FRANK.	**CAROL.**
SINGLE	OH, I'M SINGLE
CAN'T WAIT TO SWINGLE	GAWD, I'M SINGLE

FRANK.

I DON'T NEED ANYONE.

CAROL.

TABLE FOR ONE? SOUNDS LIKE FUN!

BOTH.

BECAUSE I'M SINGLE,

HOORAY, I'M SINGLE!

CAROL. *(excited) (spoken)* I'm free...to be *me*!

FRANK. *(excited) (spoken)* I'm free to be...

(suddenly dejected)

...*lonely*!

CAROL.

NO MORE DISAPPOINTMENTS

AT MY HIGH EXPECTATIONS.

FRANK.

SITTING OVER DINNER

BORED BY ALL HER RELATIONS.

CAROL.

FEEL OK WITH SAYING NO

WITHOUT FEELING GUILTY.

FRANK.

GORGING ON CANAPES,

CAROL.

THROWING OUT HIS TOUPEES.

CAROL.	**FRANK.**
SINGLE	OH, I'M SINGLE
HANG OUT A SHINGLE	I'M SO SINGLE

CAROL.

AND TELL EVERYONE YOU KNOW,

FRANK.

I'M PRIMED AND I'M SET TO GO NOW.

BOTH.

GIVE ME A JINGLE,
BECAUSE I'M SINGLE!

CAROL. *(spoken)* You go, girl!

IF I WANT THE GUYS TO DROOL
WHILE WEARING MY NAUGHTIES,
DIETING AND EXERCISE
I'M OFF TO PILATES.
SALAD BARS, NO MALLOMARS
I'M COUNTING MY CAL'RIES.
SHOULD I BE THIN FOR MEN
OR LET MYSELF GO AGAIN?

FRANK.	**CAROL.**
SINGLE	OH, I'M SINGLE
OH, GAWD, I'M SINGLE	I'M SO SINGLE

BOTH.

FORMERLY SOCIALITE,
ALONE ON A SATURDAY NIGHT.

CAROL.	**FRANK.**
BECAUSE I'M SINGLE	HI, I'M SINGLE
I NEED TO MINGLE	A RING-A-DING
DINGLE	
NEED A SOLO ROMEO	

FRANK.

I'M PRIMED AND I M SET TO GO NOW.

BOTH.

GIVE ME A JINGLE,
BECAUSE I'M SINGLE!

*(**Note on this music track:** after song ends, let track continue as one to cellphone rings.)*

*(**CAROL** exits to her offstage kitchen. **FRANK**'s cellphone rings and he takes it out of his belt clip.)*

FRANK. *(to turtle)* I'll get it!

(into cellphone)

FRANK. *(cont.)* Hello? Tom! How 'ya doin'? Great! After the day I had, I can't wait to hang out at the bar at the bowling alley tonight. We'll show all those beautiful babes what they're missing.

*(**CAROL** enters and grabs cellphone from desk.)*

CAROL. *(to goldfish)* I know, I'll call Sylvia,…find out what she's doing tonight. Maybe I'll have a ladies' night out, Bubbles!

FRANK. I'm thinking we could meet around…What?… I thought we were…

*(**FRANK** is interrupted and disappointed.)*

YOU got a DATE? How'd ya' do that?

CAROL. *(into cellphone) (pacing)* Sylvia? Hi, I got the night off from the restaurant! I thought we could go check out all those good-looking guys just waiting to meet us. I'll just freshen up and…

*(**CAROL** is interrupted and disappointed.)*

Oh, you DO? No, no problem. No, we'll take a rain check.

FRANK. Yeah, she's quite a catch…I wouldn't pass up that opportunity.

(holds cellphone away, covers mouthpiece and whispers to turtle)

I HATE him!

CAROL. So, who's the lucky guy tonight?…Oh, REALLY?

(holds cellphone to chest and whispers to fish)

That JERK! I really thought he was going to ask ME out!

FRANK. You go get 'em tiger!

(hangs up, dejected)

….HORN-DOG!

CAROL. Yes, yes, no, no, honey, I'm happy for you BOTH. Yes, you have fun tonight. OK...'bye!

(slams cellphone shut)

TRAMP!

FRANK & CAROL. Well, there goes *my* plans for tonight!

FRANK. *(to turtle)* It's just you and me, Flash.

CAROL. *(to fish)* Just you and me, Bubbles.

(CAROL exits to kitchen for wine and glass.)

FRANK. *(to Flash)* My life is crazy. Here I spend all my time trying to solve other people's financial woes, so I won't have any myself.

(patting stacks of dusty papers)

(CAROL enters with bottle of wine and wine glass.)

CAROL. *(to Bubbles)* Aw, it's just as well about tonight, I'm pooped! Some days you're the pigeon and some days you're just the statue.

FRANK. I'm just a bookkeeper cog on the paper trail of life. I think my epitaph should read, "Barely Met Expectations."

(FRANK exits to get a shaker of turtle food.)

CAROL. It's hard to be gracious for a full eight hour shift at the restaurant and still keep that big "Burger Barn" smile.

(She mugs a huge, fake smile.)

Hi, folks! Is ANYTHING all right?

(FRANK enters with shaker of turtle food.)

FRANK. How's my lovable lazy turtle?

CAROL. So how was your day, Bubbles?

FRANK. *(as if speaking to a baby)* Who's the cutest little turtle? Who's the cutest little turtle? Who's the cutest...

(Stops abruptly, realizing the turtle is motionless. He knocks on shell.)

FRANK. *(cont.)* Helloooo, anybody home? You know, buddy, you should come out of your shell sometime.

CAROL. Swish that little tail...swish...swish.

(concerned)

Same old routine, huh? Me too.

FRANK. Boy, this is all the excitement of talking to an army helmet.

CAROL. Going around in circles today? Hah, join the club.

(Both big sigh together.)

FRANK. I guess alone is better than *together* with someone you don't like.

(CUE MUSIC TRACK #3 "HAVING A PITY PARTY")

CAROL. Who am I kidding?

BOTH. I *hate* being single.

(both sing)

"PITY PARTY"

CAROL.

    I'M HAVING A PITY PARTY
    WON'T CALL FOR CELEBRATION.

FRANK.

    I'M HAVING A PITY PARTY
    I'LL SEND AN INVITATION.

CAROL.

    KNOW BEFORE YOU GET HERE,

FRANK.

    BRING YOUR OWN SEDATION,

BOTH.

    HAVIN' A PITY PARTY!

FRANK.

I'M THROWING A PITY PARTY
FROM PREVIOUS RELATIONS.

CAROL.

THROWING A PITY PARTY
I'M ENDING OLD FRUSTRATIONS.

FRANK.

LOST FRIENDS IN THE BREAKUP
'CUZ THEY RALLIED TO HER SIDE,

BOTH.

HAVIN' A PITY PARTY!

CAROL.

I HAVE NO MORE DELUSIONS.

FRANK.

I'VE BEEN STRIPPED OF ALL MY PRIDE.
TIRED OF STARTING OVER.

CAROL.

ALWAYS THE BRIDESMAID,
AND NEVER THE BRIDE.

(Both dance in their "private party.")

CAROL.

YOU KNOW HE TRIED TO CHANGE ME,
BUT THAT WAS LEFT UNSPOKEN.

FRANK.

AND HOW SHE TRIED TO FIX ME,
BUT I WASN'T BROKEN.

BOTH.

PAIN IS MY ADDICTION.
DEPRESSION WITH CONVICTION.

FRANK.

HAVIN' A PITY PARTY.

CAROL.

HAVIN' A PITY PARTY.

BOTH.

HAVIN' A PITY PARTY!

(Song ends with both slumped down in their easy chairs with glasses raised.)

FRANK. *(to turtle)* No sense in sitting around feeling sorry for myself, Flash, there's hope. Might meet someone new on a computer dating site! Just yesterday, Tom told me about "eLove" and said they *guarantee* a perfect match.

CAROL. *(to fish)* I've heard a lot of good things about this "eLove.com." There's a lot of other fish in the sea…*you* know what I'm talking about, Bubbles.

*(**FRANK & CAROL** both open up their laptop computers simultaneously.)*

FRANK. Gonna' re-boot my love life.

CAROL. OK, tonight we're gonna' get some eLove!

FRANK. *(ala booming NASCAR announcer voice)* All right, gentlemen, start your…*search* engines!

*(**FRANK & CAROL** press the power buttons on their computers at the same time, then move around their apartments preparing for an evening at home while they wait for their computers to boot up.)*

CAROL. I'm not sure I really trust the internet. I read somewhere that a third of all the men who use dating sites are already married!

FRANK. *(loudly and impatiently taps fingers on computer)* Boy, this old computer takes so long to boot up,

(shakes head)

…it's really a dinosaur,

(patting turtle's shell)

…just like you, Flash.

CAROL. But, nowadays, regular dating is so "last millennium."

FRANK. It's humiliating. Here I am paying $24 a month for high-speed rejection.

CAROL. Dating is the worst part of being single, it's like a job interview. I'd much rather date online anyway…sitting at home in front of the computer screen…in comfy clothes,

(raising wine glass)

.…with a nice glass of Merlot.

FRANK. Aww, probably better to just meet girls the old-fashioned way…drunk and falling down in a bar.

CAROL. Besides, what's the point of getting all dolled up to go out to some bar to try and impress men, who are just there to try and impress women?… When everyone will go home together and find out they weren't who they said they were in the first place.

FRANK. OK. *Finally* logged on to eLove.

CAROL. There. I've updated my anti-virus, junk-mail, hacker-spam-spyware! Now, into eLove!

FRANK. Now…screen name…

CAROL. Screen name…

FRANK. Oh, I got it!

(typing, in a low, sexy voice ala "Barry White")

…HARD DRIVE.

(smirks at his clever eName)

A little forward, but it pays to advertise.

CAROL. I really like my screen name…"Dot" Com!

FRANK. *(reading screen)* All right…sex.

CAROL. Sex.

FRANK. *(trying to make a joke to the turtle)* Not since I broke up with my "EX" three months ago.

CAROL. *(typing)* Female.

FRANK. *(to computer screen)* OK, be serious. Sex…Male.

CAROL. *(reading)* Age?

FRANK. Age?

CAROL. 30…ish?

FRANK. Ummmm…40…plus.

CAROL. 40-ish but looks 30-ish?

FRANK. 50-ish but looks 40-ish?

CAROL. Well, 40 *is* the new 30!

FRANK. Well, 50 *is* the new…48!

BOTH. *(together)* Oh, all right then…*50…ish!*

CAROL. Please fill in your physical description.

FRANK. Physical description.

CAROL. *(typing)* Healthy, average build…

FRANK. *(typing)* Athletic, good physique…

CAROL. *(to fish)* OK, maybe a few pounds over average…

FRANK. Well, I *did* work out a few times last year.

CAROL. Well, what *is* average anyway?

FRANK. *(with macho swagger)* Ruggedly handsome…

CAROL. *(typing)* And, "in shape."

    (as an aside to fish)

    Well, round *is* a shape!

FRANK. Hobbies.

CAROL. Hobbies? Umm…eating.

FRANK. Drinking…socially.

CAROL. I probably should've just borrowed a personal profile from somebody else.

FRANK. *(to turtle)* Who am I kidding? Sitting here and drinking alone is *not* socializing. Better come back to that part.

CAROL. OK, now, please list your…

BOTH. …occupation…

FRANK. Bookkeeper…

    (thoughtfully reconsidering)

    Boy, that'll really grab her attention. Wonder how fast she'll hit the delete button?

CAROL. I'm employed in the restaurant business. Nah, sounds like I'm just a waitress. I mean, I *am* the assistant manager.

FRANK. I got it. I'm an *employed* professional.

CAROL. ...in the restaurant "*industry.*"

FRANK. ...a *financial* advisor...

CAROL. *(smiling and emphatic)* Ah, a customer service representative in the "*digestive* sector!"

FRANK. OK, what's next?

CAROL. Now, to complete your personal profile, please fill in your...

BOTH. *(leaning back in chairs)* ....perfect match description.

FRANK. *(wistfully poetic to the heavens)* I'm a restless spirit. .

CAROL. Looking for a 'life connection'...

FRANK. ...who wants to explore the road less traveled...

CAROL. ...and some good conversation...

FRANK. ...with a cosmic life-partner who can see the universe in a grain of sand.

(sighs, then shakes head)

Nah, sounds like some kind of refugee from Woodstock!

CAROL. There, profile done.

FRANK. I hope this works. I've tried Romance.com, Singles.com, *Lonely* Singles.com, *Romantic* Lonely Singles.com...but no luck.

CAROL. OK, eLove...come and get me!

FRANK. Let's see if I get a hit this time.

CAROL. Here we go...

FRANK. Log on to...

(low, sexy voice)

....*LUV!*

(As if connected in time, both hit a computer button at the same instant and...)

(MUSIC TRACK #4 STARTS.
"YOU'VE GOT MAIL")

(We hear a familiar, signature voice inside the computer that says: "You've got mail!" and they both sing.)

"YOU'VE GOT MAIL"

BOTH.

> I'VE GOT MAIL.
> I'VE GOT MAIL.
> YOU'VE GOT MAIL!

> I'VE GOT MAIL.
> THE INTERNET IS TELLIN' ME
> SOMEONE KNOWS I'M HERE.

> I'VE GOT MAIL.
> THAT VOICE INSIDE MY MONITOR
> TELLS ME SOMEONE CARES.

FRANK.

> E-LOVE HAS FOUND THE PERFECT MATE.

CAROL.

> MAYBE SOMEONE WHO IS REALLY GREAT.

FRANK.

> CAME TO ME FROM OUT IN CYBER-SPACE.

CAROL.

> IT'S NOT TOO LATE,
> FOR A CYBER DATE!

CAROL. *(spoken)* It's like I found an e-Boy on e-Bay!

FRANK. *(spoken)* Computer-matched with the perfect mate. Hoo-boy! I'd love to nibble on all her Roms and Rams and Megabyte till it Mega-*Hertz*!

BOTH.

> I'VE GOT MAIL.

FRANK.
> THE INTERNET CONSIDERED
> EVERY LAST DETAIL.

CAROL.
> A CYBER-FAIRY TALE
> A PERFECT MATCH,

FRANK.
> IT'S THE DATING HOLY GRAIL.

CAROL.
> CYBER-TRONIC'LY I FOUND A MALE.

FRANK.
> INTERNET-IC'LY A HOT FE-MALE.

CAROL.
> COMPUTER MATCHED SO THIS TIME LOVE CAN'T FAIL.

BOTH.
> MY DESKTOP BROWSER IS A GREAT AROUSER.

CAROL. *(spoken)* Someone out there in cyber-space likes me. 'Mr. Right' has finally found me.

FRANK. *(spoken)* I'll find out how to turn on her… power supply.

CAROL. *(spoken)* Bet he's hard-wired.

FRANK. *(spoken)* Hope she's user-friendly.

CAROL. *(spoken)* …got good operating speed…but not *too* fast to perform!

FRANK. *(spoken)* I'll *fondle* each button…shift and "*control.*"

CAROL. *(spoken)* Better use a surge protector, just to be safe.

FRANK. *(spoken)* …and then hack into her fire-wall.

CAROL. *(spoken)* Don't want to spread around any computer viruses.

FRANK. *(spoken)* …ooh, my fingers itch to google her floppies!

FRANK.
> I'VE GOT MAIL.

CAROL.

I'VE GOT MAIL.

BOTH.

YOU'VE...GOT...MAIL!

*(**CAROL & FRANK** end number excited and hopeful.)*

CAROL. Yup, there it is, I definitely got a hit! Mr. Right's been delivered to my front door over the internet. He's Mr. Right-Now!

FRANK. OK, let's check out this perfectly computer-matched mate.

CAROL. *(reading screen excitedly)* Wow, I've been computer-matched, compatible in every category! Oh, and his screen name is "Hard Drive." Bit of an ego there, ya' think, Bubbles?

FRANK. Oh, I love her internet name, "Dot Com."... Let's just hope she's not an *"Amazon"* Dot com!

CAROL. Well, let's see how hard his drive really is. His profile says, "Employed financial professional... loves music, movies and long walks." Hmmm, long walks. Wonder if that means he doesn't own a car!?

FRANK. The digestive sector? Mmmm, well, *that's* close to my own heart.

CAROL. So, Mister "Hard Drive," tell me more about yourself. Click on *"accept match."*

FRANK. *(unnerved)* Oh, my gosh! She just popped up in my Instant Message Box! What do I do now?

CAROL. *(reading his profile)* "Cosmic life-partner?" Sounds like a refugee from Woodstock.

FRANK. OK, OK, calm down. Invite her to chat.

*(**FRANK** types in her chat name, clears throat and sits upright in the chair. Affects a big smile and a low, fake "used car salesman" voice.)*

HI!...We were just matched by eLove and you seem to be online. Wonder if you'd like to step into a chat room for some online coffee together?

CAROL. *(excited)* Oh, wow, he responded! He's online right now!

(thoughtfully)

Hmmm. We're both home, *alone,* on a Saturday night? We ARE perfectly matched! *(nervous)* OK, here goes nothing.

*(**CAROL** clears throat and affects a sexy pose and breathy voice.)*

Yes, I'm here. How "*R*"..."*U*"?

(taps single letters "R" and "U" in big, deliberate motion)

FRANK. *(taps letters "I" and "R" in big motion)* "*I*"..."*R*" fine.

(They laugh together.)

So, eLove says we seem to enjoy all the same things. Tell me more about yourself.

CAROL. Well, you've probably read my profile, so you already know a lot about me. I don't want just another intellectual connection. I'm looking for the "magic"...a spark of chemistry.

FRANK. I couldn't agree more.

CAROL. Oh, and I'm not searching for just another "cyber-friend" to chat with and exchange jokes.

FRANK. Me neither!

CAROL. OK. Now, uh, about your picture, there were five guys in it. Looked like a bowling team?

FRANK. It was. Sorry it was taken at such a distance, it was the only photo I could find.

CAROL. Which one are you?

FRANK. I'm the second pinhead from the left.

CAROL. *(squints closer to the computer screen, mutters to herself)* Talk about a "pinhead."

FRANK. And about *your* photo, I couldn't really make out your face through all those ostrich feathers and that big white hat.

CAROL. Oops, that was one of those silly Glamour Shots gone outta' control.

FRANK. Well, you have a very nice, uh...*chin.*

CAROL. I read your profile, but tell me a bit more about yourself. For example, are you a spiritual person?

FRANK. Oh, you mean what religion am I? Well, I was raised Episcopalian, you know, "Catholic-light"? All of the glory and none of the guilt.

(muttering and typing to self)

Sideways smiley face.

CAROL. *(laughs)*

FRANK. ...but I'm basically OK with ALL religions. I'd hate to blow my one shot at eternity on a *technicality.*

CAROL. *(to fish)* Oh, he's funny.

FRANK. So, tell me something personal about yourself.

CAROL. Well, I'm a recovering...shop-a-holic, currently having an out-of-money experience.

FRANK. *(they both laugh and he types)* L.O.L. Laugh-out-loud!

(to himself)

No, wait, delete that. It might look like lots-of-love.

CAROL. Even had shopper's plastic surgery,....cut up all my credit cards.

(They both laugh again.)

So, tell me some of your likes and dislikes.

FRANK. Like what?

CAROL. Oh, like what kind of music do you like?

FRANK. Well, I really like Dixieland jazz.

CAROL. Oh, like in New Orleans? Me, too! But my favorite music is the romantic love songs of the '30s and '40s.

(CUE MUSIC TRACK #5
"WE'RE ALREADY THERE")

FRANK. Like those great ballads in the classic 'black and white' movies!

CAROL. Absolutely! I've seen all the old Fred Astaire movies.

FRANK. Yeah? Well, I've seen all the *young* Fred Astaire movies.

*(**FRANK & CAROL** share a laugh together, then leave their computer desks, lost in their own thoughts as they sing.)*

"WE'RE ALREADY THERE"

CAROL.

> TO THINK I COULD HAVE LIVED MY WHOLE LIFE
> THROUGH,
> WITHOUT YOU.
> WAITING FOR A SONG, THAT I COULD SING ALONG.

FRANK.

> FOR ALL THESE DAYS AND MONTHS I MIGHT HAVE
> BEEN,
> ALL ALONE.
> WANDERING WITHOUT END, BUT MY EYES WERE
> OPENED THEN.

BOTH.

> WE'RE ALREADY THERE.

FRANK.

> SOMEHOW I WONDER IF I CLOSED MY EYES,
> I'D BE DREAMING, OF A
> LIFE I KNEW THAT COULD
> BRING A LOVE THAT'S TRUE.

CAROL.

> FOR I HAD ALWAYS HEARD THAT MIRACLES
> COULD HAPPEN
> TO SOMEONE LIKE ME, BUT IT TOOK A LIFETIME TO
> SEE.

BOTH.

> WE'RE ALREADY THERE.
> HERE WE ARE.
> WE'LL CLIMB A LITTLE HIGHER,
> MAKE THE LOAD A LITTLE LIGHTER,
> LIGHTER THAN IT'S BEEN.

CAROL.

> WE'RE ALREADY THERE.

FRANK. *(echoes)*

> WE'RE ALREADY THERE.

BOTH.

> NOW WE'RE HERE.
> WE'LL LET OUR LOVE GROW.
> AND IT'S QUITE ENOUGH TO KNOW,
> WE'RE ALREADY THERE.

CAROL.

> IT'S EASY TO LOSE HOPE FOR THE FUTURE.
> COURAGE WITHOUT END IS BROKEN.

FRANK.

> BUT I DO BELIEVE STRONGER WE WILL BE,

BOTH.

> JOINING OUR HANDS, TOGETHER WE WILL STAND.

CAROL.

> WE'RE ALREADY THERE.

FRANK. *(echoes)*

> WE'RE ALREADY THERE.

BOTH.

> NOW WE'RE HERE.
> WE'LL LET OUR LOVE GROW.
> AND IT'S QUITE ENOUGH TO KNOW,

CAROL.

> WE'RE ALREADY THERE.

FRANK. *(echoes)*

> WE'RE ALREADY THERE.

CAROL. *(echoes)*

> ALREADY THERE.

FRANK. *(echoes)*

ALREADY THERE.

BOTH.

ALREADY THERE.

*(**FRANK & CAROL** end the song in their easy chairs, then dreamily go back to their computer desks.)*

CAROL. *(startled, she notices the time clock on her computer and types)* O.M.G! Just look at the time, it's past midnight! We've been online for hours, but it just seems like minutes.

FRANK. Yeah, the time has sure flown by. It's already Sunday, but I imagine we both have the day off?

CAROL. Your imagination is perfect.

(whispers to fish)

In fact, he *sounds* perfect.

(in normal voice)

Well, I've certainly enjoyed…cyber-flirting with you.

FRANK. Likewise. And, may I say, you have beautiful… *italics.*

CAROL. Ya᾽ know, eLove promised a perfect match, and they sure delivered.

FRANK. *(sighs quietly to turtle)* Oh Flash, I think I'm falling in *"like"* with this person.

CAROL. You seem like a really nice guy.

FRANK. Well, even over the internet, I can judge that you're a very good person, too. And I can tell you, good judgment comes from experience…

(questioning in a halting way)

which, ironically, comes from a lot of bad judgment.

CAROL. You're so witty!

(mutters to herself while typing)

Sideways smiley-face. Hmmmm. Colon, dash, *double*-parenthesis.

CAROL. *(cont.)* No, wait. That kinda' looks like a double chin. Delete, delete.

FRANK. Boy, thanks to eLove, we seem to be perfectly matched.

CAROL. We do! *(stretches)* Hey, since we've been cyber-chatting for hours, why don't we take a little refreshment break, ya' know, stretch our legs?

FRANK. OK, sounds good.

CAROL. Besides, I could really go for a mega-byte of chocolate.

FRANK. Then I bid you a Swiss Fondue.

CAROL. 'Bye for now.

FRANK. 'Bye.

(mutters to self while typing)

Sideways smiley-face with ironic, semi-colon wink.

CAROL. *(mutters to self)* I just can't believe how much we have in common.

FRANK. Flash, this computer match thing really works!

CAROL. *(to fish)* We like all the same things…even down to old Fred Astaire movies and New Orleans Dix-ieland Jazz.

FRANK. This could be the relationship of my dreams and it won't take years to get to know each other. This is…

(snaps fingers)…instant compatibility!

CAROL. *(takes bite of chocolate)* Mmm. Chocolate and the internet! Love at first "BYTE!"

(back at the computer)

I'm back…are you there?

FRANK. Yes, I'm here.

CAROL. *(in a high, sing-song, flirty voice)* I missed you.

FRANK. *(surprised, turns the computer screen towards turtle)* Did you read that? She missed me! Hoo-boy! I still got the old magic! I'm getting so good at this dating thing, I could even hit on myself.

(reconsidering sarcastically)

....then, of course, later *reject* myself 'cause I'd think I could do better.

CAROL. I'm glad you're still there. I was afraid we might have lost our connection.

FRANK. Oh no, we're still connected!

CAROL. *(takes big breath)* So, I have to ask...are you *involved* with anyone right now?

FRANK. No. I dated someone for a while and eventually we wound up living together for a year.

CAROL. Did you two ever get married?

FRANK. No, we never got quite that far. But, the breakup was quite painful for both of us. How about you, were you ever married?

CAROL. No, I was never that lucky. But it wasn't for lack of trying. Out of all my relationships, the last one came the closest. But, in the end, he just couldn't commit to a permanent relationship.

FRANK. I hear a lot of *that* nowadays.

CAROL. Hey, about your "EX." Now, I know they say you shouldn't talk about previous relationships on your first online chat.

FRANK. Yeah, it's a real deal-breaker.

CAROL. *(agreeing)* All that emotional baggage from past lovers.

FRANK. *(nonchalantly)* Yeah, like who cares?!

CAROL. Yeah, tell me about it. *(impish look)* Hey, what do you say we play a little "truth or dare." I'll tell you some deep, dark secrets about *my* past, if you'll tell me some of *yours.*

FRANK. OK. But let's up the ante. What if we share secrets about former *lovers?*

CAROL. You mean our "EX's!?"

FRANK. Yeah, but let's just gossip about the most *annoying* things about our "Exes."

CAROL. *(with a devilish smile)* Oooooh! Just the things that really irritated us the most!

FRANK. Exactly. That way we'll know what we *don't* like in a person.

CAROL. OK, if you can handle it, fire away!

FRANK. Well, my "EX" was a real "*chasm*" of sarcasm.

CAROL. My "EX" was a big, boring "*blah.*"

FRANK. ...a charisma "black-hole."

CAROL. ...a bona fide jerk!

FRANK. Her moods had more swings than a trapeze artist...a regular circus act!

    (CUE MUSIC TRACK #6 "MY EX")

    (both sing)

    "MY EX"

CAROL.

    MY EX!

FRANK.

    WHAT WAS WRONG WITH YOUR EX?

CAROL. *(spoken) I* don't know where to start!

    (sings)

    TO BEGIN WITH LET'S
    TALK EGOTISTICAL,
    ANTAGONISTIC-AL,
    SURREALISTIC-AL.

FRANK.

    PAIN IN THE NECKS?

CAROL. *(nodding "yes")*

    (sings) (both hands up, cross index fingers)

    A HEX,
    I WILL PLACE ON MY EX

AND WILL VEX UPON MY
FORMERLY PREVIOUS,
SNEAKY AND DEVIOUS.

(spoken) How did you fall for *your* ex?

FRANK. *(spoken)* Beats me!

(sings)

HER COOKING COULD CURL YOUR TOES,
CONSTANTLY SHOPPED FOR CLOTHES,
DRYING HER PANTYHOSE WHILE
NAGGING ME TO PROPOSE.

HER STORIES MADE ME DOZE,
ARGUE TILL DAYBREAK ROSE,
I'VE SEEN THE PHOTOS OF
HER FORMER NOSE!

CAROL.

MY "EX,"
ALWAYS FLEXING HIS 'PECS'
WITH NO PECS TO FLEX.

IT WAS A MIRACLE, SURVIVING THAT IMBECILE
I'M SO RELIEVED HE'S MY *EX!*

FRANK.

WELL, *MY* EX!

CAROL. *(spoken)* How'd you fall for *your* "EX"?

FRANK. *(spoken)* Let me tell you...

(sings)

SHE'S THE ONE WHO'S COM-
PLEX AND MYSTERIOUS,
MOSTLY DELIRIOUS

CAROL. *(spoken)* Nice ?

FRANK. *(sings)*

ARE YOU SERIOUS?

(as an aside to himself/audience)

BUT GREAT IN BED...
AND *SEX!*

CAROL. *(Singing counter-melody with fingers in ears)*
    I DON'T CARE TO KNOW.

FRANK.	**CAROL.**
HOO-BOY! YOU TALK ABOUT SEX!	LA LA LA LA LA LA

CAROL.
    MORE THAN I WANTED TO KNOW.

FRANK.	**CAROL.**
WE WERE WRECKS, SO BELIEVE THE HYPERBOLE, SEX WAS VIAGRA-FREE. LOTSA' LATEX WITH MY EX.	LA LA LA LA LA LA

CAROL. *(spoken)* My ex was…

    (sings)

    GLUED TO HIS EASY CHAIR,
    NAIL CLIPPINGS EVERYWHERE,
    THOUGHT HE WAS DEBONAIR,
    GOD, HE WAS SUCH A SQUARE!

    FRETTING ABOUT HIS HAIR,
    SMELLING HIS UNDERWEAR, A
    SLOB WITH NO SAVOIR-FAIRE.
    I WON'T PERPLEX ON MY…

    EX!

BOTH.
    WHAT WAS UP WITH MY EX?

CAROL. *(spoken)*	**FRANK.** *(spoken)*
Got another hour?	Oh, God!

CAROL. *(sings)*
    A PRE-NUP WITH A
    POST-ADOLESCENT MIND.

FRANK.
    LOVE WAS AN UPHILL CLIMB.

CAROL.
    ENDED IT JUST IN TIME.

FRANK.

LEFT WHILE STILL IN MY PRIME.

BOTH.

HOPE THAT'S THE END OF MY *EX!*

(Music continues vamping softly under dialogue on same CD track.)

FRANK. Let me tell you a story about *my* "EX." One time, she invited me to attend her sister's wedding in New Orleans. It was during Mardi Gras and I thought it might be fun to meet all her *inbred* relatives in that goofy family of hers. I half expected the wedding band to be that banjo-playing kid from "Deliverance."

(mimics a banjo singing the "Yankee Doodle" theme [public domain] used in the film, "Deliverance")

"Ba-dah Plink-Plink-Plink-Plink-Plink-Plink-Plink"

I was mad at her 'cause I thought she was cheating on me. Well, as it turned out, I was wrong about that. I was just kinda' jealous 'cause guys were always flirting with her. Anyway, I got drunk at the reception and, yes, right in front of her *entire* family, I shot my mouth off...and accused her of being a real...

CAROL. *(interrupts realizing this story sounds familiar and just too coincidental. Matter-of-factly, but curious.)* This was in New Orleans...during Mardi Gras.

FRANK. Yup.

(music vamp fades out to silence)

CAROL. *(more curious and persistent)* Was this at Antoine's Restaurant...last *March?!*

FRANK. *(shocked pause)* Carol...IS THAT YOU?

CAROL. FRANK?

BOTH. *OH, NOOO!!!*

(blackout)

*(**IMMEDIATELY CUE MUSIC TRACK #7
"ALL YOUR FAULT"**)*

(Music intro starts immediately *during a* short *blackout of a few seconds at end of Scene 1. Stage lights up into Scene 2 just seconds later.)*

*(**Author's note:** This is also an* optional *break point for an intermission into Act II,* if *the show is presented as a Two Act musical instead of a continuous One Act.)*

ACT II

(or Scene 2 if presented continuously without intermission)

"ALL YOUR FAULT"

(fast, angry exchange of dialogue during vamp, sung in an operatic style)

CAROL. *(spoken)* You set me up!

FRANK. *(spoken)* You put me down!

CAROL. *(spoken)* I blame *you* for all this...This is all your fault!

FRANK. *(spoken) Me?* This was not *my* fault!

CAROL. *(sings)*

I THINK I KNCW THE HOUR
WHEN THINGS BEGAN TO SOUR.
THIS IS ALL YOUR FAULT!

FRANK. *(spoken)* My fault!?

(sings)

SHE BLAMES ME FOR THE BREAKUP.
WE'RE NEVER GONNA MAKE-UP.
THIS WAS NOT MY FAULT!

(He wags finger at computer.)

FRANK. *(spoken)* Oh, and about your "EX"...what was it you called me, again?...A slob?...A jerk?

CAROL. *(spoken)* Yeah, well what was all that about my *former* nose?

FRANK. *(spoken)* Oh, and I do *not* smell my underwear.

35

CAROL. *(spoken)* Well, everybody else can!

(sings)

WHEN WE BROKE UP
FROM THAT NIGHTMARE.
FINALLY WOKE UP
GLAD YOU'RE *NOT* THERE!

FRANK. *(sings)*

YOU DECEIVED ME
THEN YOU LEAVE ME.
I HAVE GRIEVED YOU DON'T BELIEVE ME.

(spoken) ...I'm offended and insulted!

CAROL. *(spoken)* Oh, how did we ever get matched up! Stupid computer! Frank, you make me so mad...

(in time with music)

I...COULD...SCREAM!

(She pantomimes scream in silence.)

VOICE-OVER. *(spoken on the pre-recorded tracks)*

In cyber-space...*no one* can hear you scream!

(They both react in horror to the demonic laugh.)

(dialogue during vamp)

CAROL. *(spoken)* I bet you planned all this!

FRANK. *(spoken)* Did not!

CAROL. *(spoken)* Did too!

FRANK. *(spoken)* I did not! It was the luck of the draw... a perfect computer match-up.

CAROL. *(spoken)* Frank, you're a real Net-Zero.

FRANK. *(spoken)* And, what does that make you...Ms. Word-Perfect?!

FRANK. *(sings)*

IT WAS SUCH A DOWNER
JUST TO BE AROUN'ER.
THAT WAS *NOT* MY FAULT!

CAROL. *(spoken)* Frank, it's always about *you.*

(sings)

I JUST NEEDED ADORATION
WITH *NO* ABBREVIATION AND
THAT WAS ALL YOUR FAULT.

FRANK. *(spoken)* Are you assigning blame to me? You're saying *your* faults were *my* fault?

CAROL. *(spoken)* I'm saying I had needs that weren't being met and you're too selfish to understand that.

FRANK. *(spoken)* Yeah, just throw it back in my face!

CAROL. *(sings)*

MARRIAGE YOU WOULD SO BELITTLE.
YOU WERE MISTER "NON-COMMITAL."

FRANK. *(sings)*

THERE ARE TWO SIDES TO EACH STORY.
YOU PASS JUDGMENT IN ALL YOUR GLORY.

CAROL. *(spoken)* This is outrageous! I don't know why I'm even communicating with you!

FRANK. *(spoken)* Carol, you make me so damned angry, I could just throw this computer right out the window.

(He starts to angrily throw laptop, but stops and pauses in the silence and quietly, lovingly embraces his laptop.)

Oh, my MAC...

CAROL. *(spoken sarcastically)* Hard drive!? More like *floppy* disc!...And I'm a, what was it again...a charisma "black hole"? Do you tell all your friends about your nagging shrew of an ex-girlfriend? Sorry I wasn't good enough for you, you *jerk!*

(sings)

THIS IS ALL YOUR DOING.
THE INTERNET YOU'RE SCREWING.

BOTH. *(on alternate words)*

> THIS IS ALL/NOT YOUR/MY FAULT!

FRANK. *(spoken)* Hard drive, how could you do this?

> *(sings)*

> COMPUTER YOU MUST HATE ME,
> LOOK HOW YOU'VE TRIED TO MATE ME.

BOTH.

> THIS IS ALL/NOT YOUR/MY FAULT!

CAROL.

> THIS IS ALL YOUR FAULT.

FRANK.

> THIS IS NOT MY FAULT.

CAROL.

> THIS IS ALL YOUR FAULT.

CAROL. *(spoken)* I don't care what you think…this is

CAROL. *(sings)*	**FRANK.** *(sings)*
ALL YOUR FAULT!	NOT MY FAULT!

> *(Song ends with them standing and pointing at their computer screens.)*

CAROL. Frank, did you really mean all those things you said about me?

FRANK. Of course not, Carol, I didn't know it was *you.*

CAROL. Well, that shouldn't have made any difference.

FRANK. Hey, we made an agreement, remember?… truth or dare. We didn't say we were going to share the *best* parts about our "Exes."

CAROL. A charisma "black-hole?" Is that how you talk about me behind my back?

FRANK. No.

CAROL. …a chasm of sarcasm?

FRANK. I was trying to be poetic. Hey, wait, what about me? I'm a bona fide *jerk?* Carol, if you can't be kind, at least have the decency to be *vague.*

CAROL. Vague!? That pretty much sums up our relationship, doesn't it? Like a jigsaw puzzle where all the pieces are *blank*.

FRANK. Well, *you* need to take some accountability. I mean, the way you always depended on the "kindness of strangers,"…it's like you had advanced "Blanche DuBois" syndrome.

CAROL. *(pointedly thoughtful)* Frank, remember when we were together, you always promised you'd die for me? Well, now that we've broken up, I think it's time you *kept* that promise!

FRANK. Ah, I see you're still annoying the world one person at a time.

CAROL. *(insistently tapping escape key)* Funny, I keep hitting the escape key on this computer, but you're *still* here!

FRANK. …and today's been so miserable, it's almost like *you're* still here!

CAROL. Frank, how could you romance me, then dump me, then romance me all over again on the internet?

FRANK. It's *my* fault the computer dating service matched us up? Carol, how could I have possibly known it was *you*?

CAROL. Yeah, well you're *still* an idiot!

FRANK. Well, of course, I'm *always* the idiot. You know, the lab results came back and I tested positive for STUPIDITY.

CAROL. Careful, Frank. You know, all that hot air contributes to global warming.

FRANK. Not when you suck all the oxygen out of the atmosphere. But, go ahead and blame me for everything.

CAROL. Yes, Frank, I *do* blame you…for our break up and for breaking my heart!

FRANK. Not this time! We were "*perfectly* matched" by a computer dating service...and that's *not* my fault!

CAROL. Oh, Frank, you could even screw up cyber-space. And what was with all that "cutesy" cyber-*foreplay* a few minutes ago? Why couldn't you be that nice when we were together?

FRANK. Oh, let me guess. Uh, because you were a bottomless well of passive-aggressive, bi-polar, neurotic, co-dependency?

CAROL. Thaaaat's right, sweet-talker, go ahead and flatter me.

FRANK. Carol, *you* made assumptions about our relationship...assumptions that one day we might get married.

CAROL. I know. How could I have been so gullible? I think my biography will be called, "Gullible's Travels."

FRANK. *(in a lecturing tone)* Carol, marriage is a hazardous thing. I mean, when you think about it, it *is* the number one cause for divorce!

CAROL. *(crying to herself with her face in hands)* Oh, why didn't I see the warning signs? The canary was in the coal mine chirping away it's last pathetic squeaks, "Run Carol run, and don't look back!"

(typing deliberately with voice of a petulant child)

Frowney-face!

FRANK. *(cooly condescending)* Carol, you went into this relationship with your eyes wide open. Hey, life is messy! Let me ask you something...Are you mad at *me?*...or are you mad at *you?*

CAROL. *(annoyed, she regains her composure)* See, Frank, that's your classic pattern...you turn things around. Look, it was never an equal partnership.

FRANK. I was just trying to be a friend to you.

CAROL. A *friend?* Is that what we were…FRIENDS? What, you wanted a *lover* at night and a *friend* during the day?

FRANK. *(dismissively)* Oh, Carol, you *knew* I loved you.

CAROL. No….No! You *never* said it! Not once. I'd say, "Frank, I love you," and you'd wink and say, "Back at 'cha, kid!"

FRANK. Well, that's my charming style.

CAROL. What a con artist! Ya' know, they say women can fake orgasms, but I think you men can fake entire relationships.

FRANK. What?

CAROL. Oh Frank, what happened to you? You used to be fun, and then…pffft!…you just ran out of fun.

FRANK. *(sadly)* I *was* fun. *(resolute)* I AM fun!

CAROL. Yeah, you were in the beginning, but towards the end, you weren't even *accessible.*

FRANK. I was just a little down because of my job. You're only blaming me now because you're thinking about the future, perhaps afraid of being alone and single?

CAROL. No, I *always* imagined it was my destiny to have a life-partner. It was never in the cards for me to be alone. I don't picture myself *by* myself.

FRANK. So what do you want from me?

CAROL. Well, for starters, I'd like you to say, "I'm sorry."

FRANK. OK…"I'm SORRY!"…that YOU can't accept any responsibility!

CAROL. Oh, Frank, what's the use of re-hashing all this? You just don't get it! Besides, your mother hated *me*, my sister hated *you*, and once the relatives got involved, the whole thing was doomed to failure.

FRANK. No, it was doomed to failure when we moved in together and OUR place was really more like YOUR place. My "stuff" was never part of *your* stuff.

CAROL. That's because you were so possessive of your "*stuff,*" that you took a Sharpie and wrote your name on everything you owned!

FRANK. And it's a good thing I did. Made it easier when we split up, didn't it?

CAROL. Oh, Frank! What did you really want from me? To show your buddies that you had a social life... with a 'trophy girlfriend?'

(She fluffs her hair in a sexy manner.)

FRANK. And what did you want from me, validation that you were attractive to men? Honestly, Carol, sometimes I just felt like I was only a "fashion accessory" to you.

CAROL. Well, if that's how you felt, why did we live together for a full year?

FRANK. Because, we enjoyed each other's *company.* We COMMUNICATED!

CAROL. COMMUNICATED? Ha! It was all one-sided! There has to be a "CO" in *CO*-MMUNICATION. We just...*MMUN*-ICATED!

FRANK. What do you mean?

CAROL. You'd ramble on and on with me just sitting there listening. I couldn't get a word in edgewise. Nothing about *us*, only about *you.*

FRANK. Hey, I let you talk...sometimes.

CAROL. LET me talk? Honestly, Frank, I think YOUR idea of good conversation is...extended monologues with *witnesses*!
(CUE MUSIC TRACK #8
"YOU NEVER LISTEN")

FRANK. Ah,...here it comes.

*(**CAROL** sings and dances with a boa-like scarf.)*
"YOU NEVER LISTEN"

CAROL.

> YOU NEVER LISTEN TO ME AT ALL.
> YOU HARDLY HEARD A THING WHEN I'D CALL.
> YOU BRAGGED ABOUT YOURSELF, GOTTA' LOTTA'
>   GALL.
> YA' THINK YOU'RE MISTER KNOW-IT-ALL. NO GIVE AND
>
> TAKE BECAUSE YOU'RE TOO HEADSTRONG.
> NO BACK AND FORTH, A SELFISH, SOLO SONG.
> YOU'RE LIKE THE PING, WITHOUT THE PONG.
> YOU NEVER LISTEN TO ME AT ALL.
>
> YOU'RE THE STEAK WITHOUT THE SIZZLE.
> YOU ARE ALKA-SELTZER, BUT YA' GOT NO FIZZLE,
> AND A DEADLY BORE TO BOOT.
> YOU ARE JUST AN EMPTY SUIT.
>
> COMMUNICATION IS NOT YOUR THING,
> AND CONVERSATION IS A SOLO FLING.
> YOU'RE LIKE THE DONG, WITHOUT THE DING.
> EVEN NOW YOU'RE NOT LISTENING.
>
> YOU'RE A GENIUS IN YOUR MIND.
> YOU NEED TO HAVE YOUR EGO REDEFINED.
> YOU ONLY LISTEN TO YOURSELF
> WHILE INTERRUPTING EVERYONE ELSE.
>
> YOU'VE GOT THE ANSWERS, BUT THEY'RE UNDER PAR.
> YOU'RE CLOSE, BUT YOU ARE NO CIGAR.
> A GAS BAG, BUFFOON AND JUST BIZARRE.
>
> I KNOW YOU KNOW I KNOW IT,
> YOUR IGNORANCE'LL SHOW IT,
> AND YOU'RE *NEVER* GONNA KNOW IT ALL!

FRANK. Boy, you *still* really have some hard feelings.

CAROL. Hey, I've nurtured this grudge for months and NO ONE is going to deprive me of it!

FRANK. Oh, Carol, don't be so *dramatic.* You know we had a good time together.

CAROL. Frank, you seem to have a convenient and selective memory,...like a goldfish. *(to fish)* Sorry, Bubbles. *(to* **FRANK***)* They say fish only have a memory of about 3 seconds. After that, "pfft," it's like nothing ever happened before in their entire life.

FRANK. So? Fish live in the moment. So what? Maybe that's the secret of happiness, living in the present and not the past.

CAROL. Frank, when we split up, it was like a heartache that wouldn't stop.

FRANK. Carol, I felt badly, too. But just think, maybe reconnecting online was meant to be. In a way, this is a blessing. All those feelings we kept inside and couldn't say in person. This allows us to get things off our chest...to clear the air through cyberspace.

CAROL. Maybe you're right. But it's hard for me to get past how you were when we broke up.

FRANK. Oh, things weren't *that* bad, were they?

(warmly)

You know, I've thought a lot about you these past three months. To be honest, I gotta' say...

CAROL. *(interrupts abruptly)* Wait, wait. To be "*honest*"? We've been chatting online for *hours* and you haven't been *honest* till *now*?

FRANK. Well, of course I have.

CAROL. I hope so. Honesty is what I expect. Besides, I seem to remember you telling me on several occasions, you *never* told a lie in your *entire* life!

FRANK. *(nonchalantly shrugs shoulders)* I was LYING!

CAROL. *(coldly)* Very funny.

FRANK. *(sarcastically)* Hey, I'm a funny guy. So, while you're at it, any *other* imperfections of mine that bother you?

CAROL. You mean outside of your *jealousy*?

FRANK. Jealousy? I've *never* been jealous of anyone in my *entire* life.

CAROL. See, you're doing it again.

FRANK. *(rolling his eyes)* So, all right. I was a little jealous back then. That's because I *cared* about you. It's a "guy" thing.

CAROL. A "*little* jealous?"

(to herself)

Who is *he* kidding? He was out of control!

(CUE TRACK #9
BACKGROUND FX "RESTAURANT NOISE")

*(Action flashback to **CAROL**'s restaurant in down-stage specials as upstage lights dim. **CAROL** is holding two menus marked "Burger Barn" and waving to a customer with a big, fake "hostess" smile.)*

CAROL. OK,....thanks for coming to Burger Barn!

FRANK. *(waves insistently at **CAROL** with a checkered napkin.)* Pssst! Carol! CAROL! Who's that guy you were talking to just now?

(He tucks napkin back under his chin.)

CAROL. Nobody. Just one of the regular customers.

FRANK. Well, you were *awfully* friendly with him.

CAROL. Frank, I have to be friendly with the customers. It's my job!

FRANK. A bit *too* friendly, if you don't mind my saying so.

CAROL. Well, I *do* mind.

(She pulls out the napkin tucked in his collar, wipes his mouth like a child, and pushes it back to him.)

FRANK. So, what did you say to him?

CAROL. I whispered in his ear...

(She looks both ways and then, in a low and breathy, sexy voice, she strikes a seductive pose.)

CAROL. *(cont.)* ....hey, big boy,...are you smoking?...or *non*-smoking?

FRANK. What?

CAROL. *(again in same sexy and breathy voice)* ....and can I get a highchair for your baby,

(big wink)

...BABY?

FRANK. Don't be ridiculous!

CAROL. *(curt and upset)* Come on, Frank, let me get back to work.

FRANK. *(defensive, feigns surprise)* I'm just saying he was giving you 'the eye.'

CAROL. He does that to every woman who works here.

FRANK. Not every woman who works here flirts with the customers like you do! Makes you look like a tramp!

CAROL. *(very angry)* Look, Frank, just finish your meal and leave...and let me do my job!

(FADE OUT FX TRACK #9)

FRANK. *(angrily)* Well, I've lost my appetite!

(CAROL throws up hands in disgust.)

(Light changes and action switches from CAROL's restaurant back to present time in the two apartments.)

FRANK. OK, so I was a jerk once or twice.

CAROL. Once or twice? What about that time in New Orleans? You *humiliated* me in front of my entire family at my sister's wedding!

FRANK. *(sheepishly)* Oh, right...the reception.

(CUE TRACK #10

BACKGROUND FX "WEDDING PARTY" NOISES WITH CONVERSATION AND CHEEZY MUSIC)

(Lights shift to downstage center specials as upstage lights dim. Action switches to a flashback of the wedding reception in New Orleans. **FRANK** *and* **CAROL** *are standing back-to-back downstage center, both holding drinks.)*

CAROL. *(adoringly)* Oh, doesn't my sister make a *beautiful* bride, all dressed in white?

FRANK. *(boorishly drunk and pointing)* Humph, with her reputation, that *broad* should be wearing plaid.

(seeming amused with himself)

CAROL. *(spins and turns directly to him)* Excuse me? What did you say?

FRANK. *(now facing her directly)* Oh, come on, your sister's been around the track more times than a Kentucky Derby winner.

CAROL. *(angrily)* Frank! You've had way too much to drink!

FRANK. Are you kidding? You can't get drunk on this cheap champagne.

CAROL. *(scolding under her breath)* Well, *you've* certainly managed to find a way.

FRANK. Look, if your tightwad family had spent some money on this shindig...paper napkins and plastic forks? I mean REALLY!

CAROL. *(apologetically to stage right, as if to a wedding guest)* Please excuse him. He doesn't get out much.

(to **FRANK** *angrily)*

Frank, *stop* it, you're embarrassing me!

FRANK. Oh, get off it, Carol. Don't be so *sanctimonious.* Look at you, the way you flirt with all the guys here at the reception. . .

CAROL. I am *not* flirting!

FRANK. *(sloppy, angry drunk)* ....you're like a bar-fight waiting to happen!

(angrily to stage left, as if to a wedding guest)

Hey buddy, what are *you* lookin' at?

(CAROL spins FRANK to her so they're nose to nose.)

CAROL. FRANK! STOP IT! You're ruining my sister's wedding.

FRANK. *(still drunk, but mean-spirited)* Yeah, what *about* your sister? She's nothin' but a high-class...

(FRANK mouthes "Horr," but never says it. He is immediately cut off by CAROL.)

CAROL. *(completes FRANK's sentence as one)* HOOORR – ible! It was *horr*-ible...

(Stage lights up immediately as they separate. They are back in present time in their apartments on their computers.)

CAROL. The things you said, Frank. How could you?

FRANK. Carol, I was *hammered*! That was the booze talking. You know I'm not that person.

CAROL. Well, that's when I threw in the towel.

FRANK. I've really changed. I've cut way back on my drinking. I'm even seeing a counselor. Carol, please forgive me.

(CUE TRACK #11
"IF WE HAD STAYED TOGETHER")

CAROL. *(showing hurt feelings, she pauses)* Frank, you pushed me away.

FRANK. And I've regretted that ever since.

(They both sing.)

"IF WE HAD STAYED TOGETHER"
("I SHOULD HAVE SEEN IT COMING")

CAROL.

> I SHOULD HAVE SEEN IT COMING,
> ALL THE WARNING SIGNS WERE THERE.
> I PRETENDED NOT TO NOTICE,
> NOW I PLAY SOLITAIRE.

FRANK.

> I SHOULD HAVE SEEN IT COMING,
> THERE WAS DISTANCE IN YOUR VOICE.
> I NOTICED IN THE SILENCE
> THERE WAS YOUR CHOICE.

BOTH.

> MAYBE WE SHOULD HAVE STAYED TOGETHER

CAROL.

> TAKE A CHANCE THAT IT WOULD LAST.

BOTH.

> MAYBE WE SHOULD HAVE STAYED TOGETHER

FRANK.

> ALWAYS HOPING IT WOULD LAST.

BOTH.

> IF WE HAD STAYED TOGETHER...

FRANK.

> I THOUGHT THIS TIME WAS DIFFERENT,
> WASN'T PLANNING FOR THE END.
> WHEN DID IT UNRAVEL?
> HOW DID I OFFEND?

CAROL.

> EXPERIENCE HAS SHOWN ME
> I'LL COME OUT THE OTHER SIDE,
>
> *(spoken)* But, damn it, I'm *exhausted.*
> *(sings)*
> AND I'M NOT SATISFIED.

FRANK.

> MAYBE WE SHOULD HAVE STAYED TOGETHER,
> KNOWING IT MIGHT NEVER LAST.

CAROL.

> MAYBE WE SHOULD HAVE STAYED TOGETHER,
> BUT THAT'S ALL NOW IN THE PAST.

BOTH.

> IF WE HAD STAYED TOGETHER,
> YOU'D BE MY LAST.

FRANK. Carol, I'm sorry we went our separate ways.

CAROL. I wish we could turn back the clock.

FRANK. We did hit it off from the very first moment we met in that cyber-café, remember?

CAROL. I'll never forget, there we were...two online-dating virgins, looking for love in cyberspace.

FRANK. And before either of us could figure out how to log on to a computer dating site…

> ### *(CUE TRACK #12*
> ### *BACKGROUND FX NOISE OF "CYBER CAFÉ")*
>
> *(As a flashback, action takes place downstage center in pool of light as upstage lights dim. FRANK and CAROL are in the cyber-cafe where they first met. We hear "coffee shop" noises with grinders and latte machines. FRANK rolls his office chair downstage center. CAROL has been working her way through an imaginary "crowded" café and spies FRANK at his "pantomime" computer. She bends to look over his shoulder and stares at his "computer screen." FRANK senses someone is there and looks suddenly over at her, startled. CAROL also reacts suddenly and gasps at being caught by surprise.)*

CAROL. *(holding hands to her chest)* Oh, I'm so sorry.

FRANK. No problem. I was so engrossed in trying to figure out how to log on to this dating site, I didn't see you.

CAROL. Oh, you're signing up with a dating site?

FRANK. Yup.

CAROL. Me, too! Your first time?

*(**FRANK** starts to reply but **CAROL** cuts him off.)*

CAROL. It's so crowded here tonight, you mind if I sit next to you?

*(**CAROL** boldly rolls her "office chair" downstage center, right next to **FRANK**.)*

FRANK. *(still taken aback)* Uh, yeah…uh, I mean, no. Uh, of course not. I've never tried this online dating thing before and…well, I'm a little nervous about it.

CAROL. *(chatty)* It's my first time, too, but apparently *everybody* is meeting online nowadays.

FRANK. I know, the computer revolution has changed history forever. We've gone from the printed page to the digital age…from paper to *vapor!*

CAROL. *(laughs)* Good point! Do you know much about computers?

FRANK. A bit…I use them at work.

CAROL. Oh, what do you do?

FRANK. I'm a bookkeeper…not very exciting really. I crunch numbers…balancing books for the unbalanced.

CAROL. No, it…sounds like steady work. Back at the restaurant I help manage, we're all just starting to learn computers.

FRANK. Well, perhaps I could help you get started logging on to your…online dating…website.

*(They pause as their eyes meet. **FRANK** extends his hand.)*

By the way, I'm Frank.

CAROL. *(smiling, shakes his hand)* .…I'm Carol. Hi!

FRANK. Nice to meet you. Uh, now…what dating site are you registered with?

CAROL. Uh, none yet. I just thought I'd google around till I found something tonight. My girlfriends tell

CAROL. *(cont.)* me that so many people meet and get married just from computer matches.

FRANK. *(thoughtfully, with a sly smile)* Say, I wonder how that would work…I mean, hypothetically, if two people met online, got married and had kids…

CAROL. …they would name them "Mac" and Pee-Cee!

FRANK. *(laughs)* Yeah, and the parents could say they met googling and giggling online…

CAROL. …and then snuck into a secluded chat room one night and *(as a cowboy yell)* ….YA-*HOOOO*!!"

FRANK. *(animated and laughing along with* **CAROL***)* And since neither one had used a "fire-wall," it was too late to hit the delete button…

CAROL. *(finishing his sentence)* ….so, nine months later, a little "pop-up" appeared that said…

BOTH. *(pointing to pantomime computer and mimicking a "computer voice")*
….."YOU'VE GOT…A MALE!"

(Both laugh, look at each other and realize their chemistry together.)

FRANK. Say, you're a lot of fun.

CAROL. So are you.

FRANK. *(pointing enthusiastically)* Oh, let's check out this dating site. "Hot Girls and Cool Guys…Seniors' Edition."

CAROL. Oh, let me see.

FRANK. *(mimes turning monitor away, making up a profile)* No, no. I'll read it. Oh, here's one for me.
FOXY OLDER LADY: Sexy, fashion-conscious, blue-haired beauty, slim, 5'4"…used to be 5'6," searching for older, sharp-dressing companion. Matching white shoes and belt a plus. Let's meet, take out our hearing aids and share quiet times together.

CAROL. *(looks at him questioningly, then realizes he's kidding)* It doesn't say that!

(mimes turning monitor to her and makes up a profile)

Oh, here's one for me!

HIGH-MILEAGE 1932 MALE: Good condition. Lotsa' new parts including…hip, knee, cornea and valves. Seeks classic female who values vintage models with experience…nursing degree a plus.

FRANK. Oh, come on, you made that up.

CAROL. *(laughs)* Yeah, but we shouldn't laugh, these might be *our* profiles in a few more years.

FRANK. Hey…what are you doing tonight?

CAROL. I don't know, why?

FRANK. Wanna' go dancing?

CAROL. Dancing?

FRANK. You know, like Fred Astaire and Ginger Rogers? What a couple they were.

CAROL. Oh, I don't know. I'm pretty rusty.

FRANK. Oh, come on. Fred was always so suave and debonair. He made getting the girl look so easy.

(CUE MUSIC TRACK #13
"I WAS MEANT FOR YOU")

(he sings)

"I WAS MEANT FOR YOU"

FRANK.

SOMETIMES I PONDER AS I WANDER THINKING OF YOU,
I GROW FONDER OF THE THINGS YOU DO.
OUR HEARTS WILL MEET IF THE FATES ALLOW,
BUT THIS IS WHAT MY HEART TELLS ME RIGHT NOW,

I WAS MEANT FOR YOU AND YOU WERE MEANT FOR ME.
CAN'T YOU SEE HOW LUCKY WE COULD BE?
YOU WERE MEANT FOR ME AND I WAS MEANT FOR YOU.

FRANK. *(cont.)*

> I PROPOSE THERE'S SOMETHING WE CAN DO.
> WE'LL FLY THROUGH THE AIR ON A TRIP TO PARADISE.
> TO SHARE WITHOUT CARE WOULD BE AWFUL NICE,
> SO MY ADVICE IS...
>
> I WAS MEANT FOR YOU AND YOU WERE MEANT FOR ME.
> COME WITH ME, HOW HAPPY WE WILL BE.

> *(**FRANK** and **CAROL** dance together as part of the cyber-cafe flashback.)*

FRANK. *(spoken during instrumental)* Yeah, good old Fred Astaire...Mr. Smoothie. Made everything look easy. So maybe a little romance isn't such a bad thing after all.

> *(continues singing)*

> WE'LL FLY THROUGH THE AIR ON A TRIP TO PARADISE.
> TO SHARE WITHOUT CARE WOULD BE AWFUL NICE,
> SO MY ADVICE IS...
> I WAS MEANT FOR YOU AND YOU WERE MEANT FOR ME
> COME WITH ME, HOW HAPPY WE WILL BE.

> *(Song ends as they dance apart and back to their own sides of the stage, in their apartments.)*

CAROL. *(talking to herself)* Oh, why is this man back in my life again...

> *(wistfully looking into computer screen)*

...floating out there in cyber-space?

FRANK. *(to himself)* Boy, we really did have something.

> *(typing to her)*

You know, honey, this may sound crazy, but I think I still love you.

CAROL. *(sees screen and points in surprise)* He said it! He *actually* said it!

> *(to fish)*

Well, he *wrote* it, anyway. Funny, he never could say it out loud in person when we were together.

(CUE MUSIC TRACK #14
"JUST A DREAM")

CAROL. *(music intro starts as she takes out a photo of them together)* I guess there's a kind of safe distance over the internet.

(she sings)

"JUST A DREAM"

CAROL. *(singing to a photo of them together)*
WE FELL IN LOVE AND
YOU WERE LIKE A DREAM TO ME,
SO NEAR AND YET SO FAR AWAY.

I HELD YOU IN MY HEART
BUT NEVER HEARD YOU SAY,
YOU LOVED ME, TOO,
UNTIL TODAY.

AND ALL ALONG
I HEARD A DISTANT SONG
THAT SAID THAT WE WERE MEANT TO BE,

BUT MY DREAMS OUT THERE,
FLOATING IN THE AIR,
ASKING, ARE YOU REAL?
ARE YOU TRULY THERE?

HOW CAN I HOLD YOU CLOSE
WHEN YOU HAVE ALWAYS SEEMED
SO NEAR AND YET SO FAR AWAY?

YOU CAME INTO MY LIFE AGAIN,
MY DREAMS WOULD SAY, THAT
NOW WE FIND, THAT
LOVE IS BLIND,
SO NEAR, YET FAR AWAY.

CAROL. *(sighs thoughtfully)* It makes no sense to still have feelings for him again. And now, suddenly, love walks back in through a door you never even knew you left open.

FRANK. *(types in)* Carol,…are you still there?

CAROL. *(she types back)* I'm here.

(wistfully)

Hey,…what are you thinking right now?

FRANK. I was thinking about the first moment I knew I loved you.

CAROL. *(thoughtful pause)* Frank, do you think you were *afraid* of love?

FRANK. Well, people get hurt.

CAROL. That's the risk you take. Maybe you were just afraid of your feelings.

FRANK. No…I was afraid of *your* feelings.

CAROL. And now you're worried about *our* feelings.

FRANK. *(smiles wistfully)* You know the thing I loved *most* about living with you?

CAROL. What's that?

FRANK. Every night, you were the last person I saw before I'd dream…and the first person I saw when I awoke.

(Looking out his window, faint rays of sunlight appear in his apartment.)

Hey, look, it's almost daylight. We've been online all night! See out there? The beginning of a new day. Maybe a day where we could…start over?

CAROL. Perhaps.

FRANK. Go ahead, look out your window.

(CUE MUSIC TRACK #15
"A SUNRISE LULLABY")

(FRANK and CAROL move downstage looking out imaginary windows as they sing.)

"LOVE WILL HAVE A NEW DAY"

FRANK.

> THE DAWN OF A BRAND NEW DAY
> SHINES LIKE THE HOPE IN THE SUN'S BOUQUET
> WITH MOTHER OF PEARL AND BRIGHT PURE GOLD,
> LOVE WILL HAVE A NEW DAY.
>
> LOVE HAS A BRAND NEW DAY,
> STARTING ANEW WITH THE SUN'S FIRST RAY.
> SINGING A SUNRISE LULLABY,
> LOVE HAS A SHINING NEW DAY.

CAROL. *(spoken)* You know, Frank, back when we were still in love, I imagined how I wanted to see *my* final sunrise.

FRANK. *(spoken)* Really? How's that?

CAROL. *(spoken)* Oh, years from now, when my time had come, and I had seen all the sunrises I was ever meant to see…I wanted to enter eternity laughing…wrapped up in *your* arms.

FRANK.

> THE DAWN OF A BRAND NEW DAY

CAROL.

> SHINES LIKE THE HOPE IN THE SUN'S BOUQUET.

BOTH.

> SINGING A SUNRISE LULLABY,
> LOVE HAS A SHINING NEW DAY.

FRANK.

> WE'RE NOT ON THIS ROAD ALL ALONE.
> WE'RE ALL ON A JOURNEY TRAVELIN' HOME.

BOTH.

> SO OPEN YOUR HEART TO THIS SUNRISE BOUQUET,
> AND LOVE WILL HAVE A NEW DAY.

FRANK.	**CAROL.**
IN THE FIRST LIGHT OF SUN,	
THE SILENCE OF THE DAWN,	OOO *(on word,*
MY HEART HAS FOUND A	*"dawn")*
GOAL.	OOO

CAROL.
> LOVE EVERY DAY
> CAN MEND A BROKEN HEART,
> AND SEE THROUGH
> THE WINDOW OF YOUR SOUL.

BOTH.
> AND LOVE WILL START A NEW DAY.

FRANK. Carol, let's try and put all the hurt behind us.

CAROL. And make a brand new start?

FRANK. You only live once…and you never want to live with regret.

CAROL. Frank, I didn't really mean all those things I said about you.

FRANK. Me neither. Carol, we might have made a terrible mistake in breaking up and eLove is…

BOTH. *(simultaneously)* ….giving us a second chance.

FRANK. *(with a warm smile)* Right.

CAROL. Well, at least we got a few good laughs out of revisiting our past miseries tonight.

FRANK. We got a lot of things off our chest.

CAROL. You can say that again.

FRANK. We got a lot of things off our chest.

CAROL. Oh, Frank!

FRANK. So, how about a date?

CAROL. A DATE? You don't have a date with your "EX" that you just broke up with!

FRANK. OK, then we'll call it a *blind* date. We'll cover our eyes and pretend we don't know each other.

CAROL. *(chuckles)* Oh, Frank, you always *could* make me laugh.

FRANK. Told ya'. I AM funny.

> *(CUE WALTZ MUSIC TRACK #16*
> *REPRISE OF "I'M SINGLE")*

CAROL. *(smiling)* Oh…all right then.

> (**CAROL** *and* **FRANK** *sing, "dancing" alone around in their desk chairs and whirling around their apartments.*)

> ### *"I'M SINGLE"*
> ### *(WALTZ REPRISE)*

CAROL.

HI THERE, I'M SINGLE.

FRANK. *(spoken)* Hi!

> *(sung)*

YOU WANNA' MINGLE?

CAROL.

WALTZING THROUGH CYBER-SPACE

FRANK.

WITH A BIG SMILEY-FACE.

ALTHOUGH I'M SINGLE,

CAROL.

I FEEL A TINGLE,

FRANK.

DANCING LIKE FRED ASTAIRE,

CAROL.

WHAT A BREATH OF FRESH AIR.

CAROL.

I MUST CONFESS TO SOME FASCINATION

FRANK.

IN THE MIDST OF THIS ODD SITUATION,

BOTH.

WE'VE RETURNED TO OUR FORMER FIXATION,

CAROL.

MATCHING THE SAME MATCH,

FRANK.

CATCHING THE SAME CATCH.

CAROL.	FRANK.
(sings melody)	*(sings counter-melody)*
WITH THIS SINGLE	I'M SO SINGLE
A FLAME TO REKINDLE	OH, SO SINGLE

BOTH.

FALLING IN LOVE AGAIN
FOR THE VERY FIRST TIME,
COME, LET'S CO-MINGLE
SO WE WON'T BE SINGLE.

FRANK.

SINGLE.

CAROL.

NOT SINGLE.

BOTH.

TOGETHER WE'RE SINGLE NO MORE.

CAROL. Frank, I've missed you.

FRANK. And *I've* missed you. Carol,...do you think you could warm up to the idea of getting back together? Just kinda'...*marinate* on it.

CAROL. Well, in a world that allows internet dating, I guess anything's possible.

FRANK. So, it's a date! Uh, where do you live now?

CAROL. Oh, I moved into an apartment just a block North of that cyber-café where we first met.

FRANK. *(rolls eyes and chuckles)* Carol, I live a few blocks just SOUTH of that same coffee shop!

CAROL. *(laughs and points at screen)* You're a cyber-stalker, that's what you are!

FRANK. *(chuckles)* So, we'll meet at the same cyber-café where we first met.

CAROL. OK...when?

FRANK. How 'bout...well, how about right now?

CAROL. *(indicating to time on computer screen)* Frank, it's 5 o'clock in the morning!

FRANK. So? That coffee shop is open 24 hours now, even on Sunday mornings…and besides, we have to "Carpe the ol' Diem."

CAROL. …and live in the moment!

FRANK. Right. Besides, this exact moment in time will never, ever happen again for all eternity. So what are we waiting for?

CAROL. *(sighs)* Oh,…OK. I'll get my coat and meet you down the block. Just for *coffee*…for *old* time's sake.

FRANK. …for *new* time's sake.

CAROL. …for *good* time's sake.

FRANK. And hey, who knows? We *both* might get lucky!

CAROL. *(shakes head, smiles and rolls her eyes)* I'll see ya' in a minute…'*bye.*

(**FRANK** *and* **CAROL** *both slowly and simultaneously close their laptop computers.*)

FRANK. I can't believe it, I just made a blind date with my "EX." They oughta' write a musical about this.

(stops, looks directly at audience and shakes head)

Naaah…no one would ever believe it.

CAROL. *(sighs and picks up a photo of the two of them together)* Oh, well, here goes a second chance at romance.

FRANK. *(to turtle, rubbing his shell)* Wish me luck, Flash. Wish me luck? What would you know? You're like the poster-boy for

(he chuckles)

…a *reptile* dysfunction.

(to himself straightening his collar in downstage "mirror")

Ha-ha-hah.

(resolutely serious)

See? I *am* still funny.

(They both dance easily around their apartments getting ready to go out. **FRANK** *sings a short acappella reprise of the song, "I Was Meant for You.")*

(sings and hums)

FRANK. I WAS MEANT FOR YOU, AND YOU WERE MEANT FOR ME...

CAROL. *(hums along later in the phrase)* Oh, he *did* make me laugh and I *do* miss the laughing...

FRANK. And I *do* miss the sex...

CAROL. *(a suggestive look)* ...and we *were* good in bed, especially the part where we would...

(smiles and shakes head)

...watch old Fred Astaire movies and eat popcorn.

FRANK. Well, here goes nothing...or maybe everything.

(CUE MUSIC TRACK #17
SLOW AD LIB REPRISE OF "MY EX")

*(**NOTE:** after song, this CD track segues directly into the "bow music" as one.)*

(they sing)

"MY EX" (AD LIB REPRISE)

FRANK.

MY EX,...JUST MADE A DATE WITH MY EX.

CAROL.

THIS SEEMS IMPOSSIBLE,

FRANK.

HIGHLY IMPROBABLE,

CAROL.

DOWNRIGHT INCREDIBLE.

BOTH.

I'LL COME FACE TO FACE WITH MY EX.

FRANK.

WE MIGHT HAVE "MAKE-UP" SEX.

CAROL.

PAST INSULTS WE'LL ACQUIT,

FRANK.

THE FUTURE'S INDEFINITE,

CAROL.

A DATE DOESN'T MEAN COMMIT.

BOTH.

WHO'DA' BELIEVED IT? I'M HAVING A DATE WITH MY...

(spoken together in open break of music, standing in their open doorway)

....*EX!*

(Both close their apartment doors simultaneously in tempo to the closing "bump" note of music.)

(blackout)

(They both exit out their upstage front doors, dressed in outdoor attire on the way to their "blind dates" for an early-morning coffee.)

(The exit blackout lasts only a few seconds and restores to full stage wash at the beginning of the "Bow Music" as both actors re-enter through their respective front doors.)

*(**BLACKOUT AND ROUSING BOW MUSIC OF**) **"MY EX – BOWS"***

(IMPORTANT NOTE!!! ***TRACK #17 "MY EX" (AD LIB REPRISE)*** *SEGUES DIRECTLY INTO THE BOW MUSIC. DO NOT STOP TRACKS!!)*

(Author's suggestion for staging bows:) *(Both actors emerge from their apartment front doors simultaneously, take a bow together then individually [**CAROL** first]. They both gesture to the tech booth and then to their respective pets. They bow again and start to exit through their front doors then briefly stop, look at each other, hold hands to mouth pantomiming a "telephone" and mouth "call me," then exit.)*

The End

PROPERTY LIST

2 laptop computers
2 computer desks
2 computer chairs with wheels
2 different easy chairs
2 cell phones
2 photo frames with photo of Frank & Carol together
Hat rack (**FRANK**)
Fred Astaire movie poster framed (**CAROL**)
Dixieland jazz poster framed (**FRANK**)
Small fishbowl with one prop (or live) goldfish (**CAROL**)
Fish food shaker (**CAROL**)
Turtle terrarium or dish with low sides(**FRANK**)
Turtle food shaker (**FRANK**)
Prop turtle shell or painted rock (**FRANK**)
2 bags of groceries
2 sets of house keys
Small stack of mail (**CAROL**)
Soap opera magazine or tabloid papers (**CAROL**)
Wine glass (**CAROL**)
Bottle of Merlot filled with grape juice mixture (**CAROL**)
Generic drinking glass (**FRANK**)
Bottle of tequila (**FRANK**)
Sodas (**FRANK**)
Bag of small chocolates individually wrapped (**CAROL**)
Dish for chocolates (**CAROL**)
Bag of pre-microwaved popcorn (**CAROL**)
Pringles can or bag of potato chips(**FRANK**)
Office cardboard boxes and paperwork (**FRANK**)
Adding machine (**FRANK**)
2 menus marked "Burger Barn" (**CAROL**)
1 napkin – red or blue checkered (**FRANK**)

SOUND EFFECTS
(Note: all sounds are *included* on music CD tracks)
Cellphone rings
Background restaurant sounds
Background wedding party sounds
Background coffee house sounds
Voice over: "You've got mail!"
Voice over: "In cyberspace no one can hear you scream.
(laugh)"

COSTUMES

CAROL:
Light weight coat
Blouse – upscale for work
Slacks
Vest
Scarf/boa-like
Purse
Robe
Pumps – for work
Low heeled shoes/slippers that Carol can dance in

FRANK:
Overcoat or Raincoat
Sport jacket
Shirt – button down for work
Tie
Slacks
Fedora hat
Shoes – for both work and comfort
Robe

"eLove" SHOW PERFORMANCE CD MUSIC TRACKS – CUE SHEET

TRACK #1 – SUNRISE LULLABY (instrumental intro)

TRACK #2 – I'M SINGLE (includes Overture & cellphone ring)

TRACK #3 – PITY PARTY

TRACK #4 – YOU'VE GOT MAIL

TRACK #5 – WE'RE ALREADY THERE

TRACK #6 – MY EX

TRACK #7 – IT'S ALL YOUR FAULT

TRACK #8 – YOU NEVER LISTEN

TRACK #9 – Background "Restaurant" sound FX

TRACK #10 – Background "Wedding Party" sound FX

TRACK #11 – IF WE HAD STAYED TOGETHER

TRACK #12 – Background "Coffee House" sound FX

TRACK #13 – YOU WERE MEANT FOR ME

TRACK #14 – JUST A DREAM

TRACK #15 – SUNRISE LULLABY

TRACK #16 – I'M SINGLE – REPRISE WALTZ

TRACK #17 – MY EX – REPRISE & BOW MUSIC

TRACK #18 – ALL YOUR FAULT (THEME) – THEATRE EXIT MUSIC

NOTE: 6 SECOND SPACE ONLY AFTER EACH TRACK

"eLove" SONG CREDITS FOR PROGRAM

1. LOVE HAS A BRAND NEW DAY (intro)
   Music and Lyrics by Wayland Pickard (ASCAP)

2. I'M SINGLE
   Music by Wayland Pickard (ASCAP)
   Lyrics by Wayland Pickard (ASCAP) & Sherry Netherland
   (ASCAP)

3. PITY PARTY
   Music by Wayland Pickard (ASCAP)
   Lyrics by Wayland Pickard (ASCAP) & Sherry Netherland
   (ASCAP)

4. YOU'VE GOT MAIL
   Music by Wayland Pickard (ASCAP)

5. WE'RE ALREADY THERE
   Music by Wayland Pickard (ASCAP)
   Lyrics by Deborah Johnson (ASCAP)

6. MY EX
   Music by Wayland Pickard (ASCAP)
   Lyrics by Wayland Pickard (ASCAP) & Sherry Netherland
   (ASCAP)

7. IT'S ALL YOUR FAULT
   Music by Wayland Pickard (ASCAP)
   Lyrics by Wayland Pickard (ASCAP) & Sherry Netherland
   (ASCAP)

8. YOU NEVER LISTEN
   Music and Lyrics by Wayland Pickard (ASCAP)

9. IF WE HAD STAYED TOGETHER
   Music by Wayland Pickard (ASCAP)
   Lyrics by Wayland Pickard (ASCAP) & Sherry Netherland
   (ASCAP)

10. I WAS MEANT FOR YOU
    Music and Lyrics by Wayland Pickard (ASCAP)

11. SO NEAR YET SO FAR AWAY
    Music and Lyrics by Wayland Pickard (ASCAP)

12. LOVE HAS A BRAND NEW DAY (A SUNRISE LULLABY)
    Music and Lyrics by Wayland Pickard (ASCAP)

13. I'M SINGLE – REPRISE WALTZ
    Music and Lyrics by Wayland Pickard (ASCAP)

14. MY EX – AD LIB REPRISE
    Music by Wayland Pickard (ASCAP)
    Lyrics by Wayland Pickard (ASCAP) & Sherry Netherland
    (ASCAP)

"eLove" STAGE PLOT

CAROL'S APARTMENT

FRANK'S APARTMENT

EXIT OFFSTAGE

Freestanding Flat

Movie Poster

Easy Chair

Side Table

Side Stand

Door

Desk

Rolling Desk Chair

Bookcase

Tape Line

Desk

Rolling Desk Chair

Bookcase

Door

Side Stand

EXIT OFFSTAGE

Hatrack

Side Chair

Freestanding Flat

ABOUT THE PLAYWRIGHT

WAYLAND PICKARD is a Cine Golden Eagle Film Award-Winner, an HBO Television "Ace" Award Nominee and Billboard Songwriting Finalist. He won the Los Angeles 2008 ADA Best Director Award and was the 2006 ADA Award winner for Best Actor (LA Valley Theatre League). A national recording artist and 2009 Grammy Award contender, he's scored music for film and television plus recorded five albums. He wrote a musical with Phil Olson entitled *Polyester* also published by Samuel French. He performs as a headliner at concert halls throughout the country. Find out more by visiting www.WaylandPickard.com and www.eLoveTheMusical.com.

OTHER TITLES AVAILABLE FROM SAMUEL FRENCH

POLYESTER - THE MUSICAL

Book by Phil Olson
Music by Wayland Pickard
Lyrics by Phil Olson and Wayland Pickard

3m, 2f / Musical Comedy

The story of The Synchronistics, an over-the-hill ABBA wannabe group that reunites after 20 years to perform at a public access TV telethon, put their differences aside, and try to save the station from going under.

The year was 1979 and The Synchronistics were big. Big enough to be on Johnny Carson. Their hit single, "Better Together" rose to number two on the Billboard Charts. Then something terrible happened that drove the group apart. And now, 20 years later, they're back together in Maple Valley, their home town, to perform at the 1999 WKLN public access TV Telethon.

Will they overcome their differences from 20 years ago, act professionally and help save WKLN from going under? Probably not. But you never know what to expect when this dysfunctional group gets together...one last time.

It's "*Mamma Mia*" meets "*Spinal Tap*"

Featuring 16 original songs including
"The Funk Train" and "Bump Your Booty Rump."